Geronimo Stilton

ENGLISH!

21 FREE TIME 課餘時間

新雅文化事業有限公司

www.sunya.com.hk

Geronimo Stilton English
FREE TIME　課餘時間

作　　者：Geronimo Stilton 謝利連摩·史提頓
譯　　者：申倩
責任編輯：王燕參
封面繪圖：Giuseppe Facciotto
插圖繪畫：Claudio Cernuschi, Andrea Denegri, Daria Cerchi
內文設計：Angela Ficarelli, Raffaella Picozzi
出　　版：新雅文化事業有限公司
　　　　　香港英皇道499號北角工業大廈18樓
　　　　　電話：（852）2138 7998
　　　　　傳真：（852）2597 4003
　　　　　網址：http://www.sunya.com.hk
　　　　　電郵：marketing@sunya.com.hk
發　　行：香港聯合書刊物流有限公司
　　　　　香港新界大埔汀麗路36號中華商務印刷大廈3字樓
　　　　　電話：（852）2150 2100　傳真：（852）2407 3062
　　　　　電郵：info@suplogistics.com.hk
印　　刷：C & C Offset Printing Co.,Ltd
　　　　　香港新界大埔汀麗路36號
版　　次：二〇一二年七月初版
　　　　　10 9 8 7 6 5 4 3 2 1

ISBN: 978-962-08-5548-1
© 2008 Edizioni Piemme S.p.A., Via Tiziano 32 - 20145 Milano - Italia
International Rights © 2007 Atlantyca S.p.A. - via Leopardi, 8, Milano - Italy
© 2012 for this Work in Traditional Chinese language, Sun Ya Publications (HK) Ltd.
18/F, North Point Industrial Building, 499 King's Road, Hong Kong.
Published and printed in Hong Kong

CONTENTS
目 錄

BENJAMIN'S CLASSMATES　班哲文的老師和同學們　4

GERONIMO AND HIS FRIENDS　謝利連摩和他的家鼠朋友們　5

THE TELEPHONE IS RINGING　電話響了　6

HELLO, WHO'S SPEAKING?　喂，你是哪位？　8

THE SCHOOL PLAY　學校話劇　10
A SONG FOR YOU! - Ball of the Queen of the Fairies

THE MUSICAL　音樂劇　12

THE ROCK CONCERT　搖滾演唱會　14

LET'S GO TO THE CINEMA!　一起去看電影！　16

AT THE NATURAL SCIENCE MUSEUM　自然科學博物館　18
A SONG FOR YOU! - At the Museum

FREE TIME IS HARD WORK　休息時間變了艱苦工作 　20

TEST　小測驗　24

DICTIONARY　詞典 　25

GERONIMO'S ISLAND　老鼠島地圖　30

EXERCISE BOOK　練習冊

ANSWERS　答案

BENJAMIN'S
CLASSMATES
班哲文的老師和同學們

Maestra Topitilla
托比蒂拉·德·托比莉斯

Rarin
拉琳

Diego
迪哥

Rupa
露芭

Tui
杜爾

David
大衛

Sakura
櫻花

Mohamed
穆哈麥德

Tian Kai
田凱

Oliver
奧利佛

Milenko
米蘭哥

Trippo
特里普

Carmen
卡敏

Atina
阿提娜

Esmeralda
愛絲梅拉達

Pandora
潘朵拉

Takeshi
北野

Kuti
菊花

Benjamin
班哲文

Hsing
阿星

Laura
羅拉

Kiku
奇哥

Antonia
安東妮婭

Liza
麗莎

GERONIMO AND
HIS FRIENDS
謝利連摩和他的家鼠朋友們

謝利連摩·史提頓 Geronimo Stilton
一個古怪的傢伙，簡直可以說是一隻笨拙的文化鼠。他是
《鼠民公報》的總裁，正花盡心思改變報紙業的歷史。

菲·史提頓 Tea Stilton
謝利連摩的妹妹，她是《鼠民公報》的特派記者，同
時也是一個運動愛好者。

班哲文·史提頓 Benjamin Stilton
謝利連摩的小姪兒，常被叔叔稱作「我的
小乳酪」，是一隻感情豐富的小老鼠。

潘朵拉·華之鼠 Pandora Woz
柏蒂·活力鼠的姨甥女、班哲文最好的朋友，
是一隻活潑開朗的小老鼠。

柏蒂·活力鼠 Patty Spring
美麗迷人的電視新聞工作者，致力於她熱愛的電視事業。

賴皮 Trappola
謝利連摩的表弟，非常喜歡食物，風趣幽默，是一隻饞
嘴、愛開玩笑的老鼠，善於將歡樂傳遞給每一隻鼠。

麗萍姑媽 Zia Lippa
謝利連摩的姑媽，對鼠十分友善，又和藹可親，只想將
最好的給身邊的鼠。

艾拿 Iena
謝利連摩的好朋友，充滿活力，熱愛各項運動，他希望
能把對運動的熱誠傳給謝利連摩。

史奎克·愛管閒事鼠 Ficcanaso Squitt
謝利連摩的好朋友，是一個非常有頭腦的私家
偵探，總是穿着一件黃色的乾濕樓。

THE TELEPHONE IS RINGING
電話響了

親愛的小朋友，你知道我有多麼以我的小姪兒班哲文為榮嗎？他和潘朵拉將會在學校的話劇演出中當主角！當柏蒂打電話邀請我一起去看時，我興奮極了！

pass the word round
把消息傳開去

Of course!

Ok, Patty! See you this afternoon!

跟我謝利連摩·史提頓一起學英文，
就像玩遊戲一樣簡單好玩！

你可以一邊看着圖畫一邊讀。
以下有幾個標誌，你要特別留意：

當看到 標誌時，你可以聽CD，
一邊聽，一邊跟着朗讀，還可以跟
着一起唱歌。

當看到 ★ 標誌時，你可以和朋友
們一起玩遊戲，或者嘗試回答問
題。題目很簡單，它們對鞏固你所
學過的內容很有幫助。

當看到 標誌時，你要注意看一
下格子裏的生字，反覆唸幾遍，掌
握發音。

最後，不要忘記完成小測驗和練習
冊裏的問題！看看你有多聰明吧。

祝大家學得開開心心！

謝利連摩·史提頓

HELLO, WHO'S SPEAKING?
喂，你是哪位？

我實在壓抑不住興奮的心情！於是馬上打電話通知親戚和朋友們。

The kids are acting…
孩子們在演出……

Are you coming to see them?
你會來看他們嗎？

Hello, who's speaking?
1

Hi, Trappola, it's me, Geronimo!

2

Hi, Geronimo, how are you?
3

4

I'm fine, thanks, and you?

5

Not bad. It's nice to hear from you!

6

The kids are acting in a school play this afternoon. Are you coming to see them?

10

Bye!

Ok, see you later. Bye!

Well, then... see you there.

I think so. Of course, I'll be there!

9

8

7

8

當大家接到我的電話，他們的興致都很高！每隻鼠都想參加。我以一千塊莫澤雷勒乳酪發誓，這可是千載難逢的好機會啊！

You must come, you can't miss it...

Ok, I think I can come. I'll be there at four thirty, ok?

So, Aunt Lippa, I'll save a place next to mine, ok?

Yes, thank you Geronimo!

Please, try not to be late, as usual.

Don't worry, I'll be on time!

 試用英語説出：「可以的，我想我能去。」

答案：*Ok, I think I can come.*

THE SCHOOL PLAY
學校話劇

小朋友們都迫不及待要開演了。托比蒂拉老師一邊幫他們整理服飾，一邊給他們作最後的提點。布幕馬上就要拉開了，好緊張啊！

defeated
打敗
became
成為

THE ENCHANTED FOREST

scene, set

lights, spotlights

crown　queen

dancer　script　pixie

king

witch　spirit of the forest　costu

Whose is this costume?

ghost

It's mine!

mask　fairy　make-

10

我以一千塊莫澤雷勒乳酪發誓，要記住所有台詞真不容易呢！幸好，孩子們在上台表演前已經排演過很多遍了。

A long time ago, everybody was happy in the kingdom of imagination. The king and the queen were wise and generous.

One day, the witch cast a spell on them, and everybody fell asleep. The country became a large enchanted forest.

Only fairies, pixies, ghosts and the spirits of the forest were awake, but they were sad.

One day, the queen of the fairies defeated the witch and happiness returned to that country!

A SONG FOR YOU!

Track 1

Ball of the Queen of the Fairies

Kings, queens, pixies and fairies, they only live in the kingdom of imagination.

Come to the ball of the queen of the fairies in the enchanted forest in the kingdom of imagination!

THE MUSICAL 音樂劇

除了話劇外，班哲文和潘朵拉也很喜歡音樂劇。當柏蒂提出要帶他們去看音樂劇時，他們都很開心！柏蒂還邀請我一起去呢。

> have fun
> 玩得開心

試用英語說出：「我預訂了四個劇院的位子。」

答案：I booked four seats at the theatre.

到了劇院，排隊買票的鼠很多，幸好柏蒂已經預訂了門票，否則我們可能沒有位子了。

Patty: Good evening, I booked four tickets over the phone.

Cashier: Your name, please.

Patty: Patty Spring!

Cashier: Yes, here they are. You are in the first row. 600 dollars all together.

Patty: 600 dollars, here you go. Thank you.

Cashier: Thank you! Enjoy yourselves!

! Fun, isn't it?
很有趣，不是嗎？

They are in the first row, central seats, 13, 14, 15 and 16!

What number are our seats?

Fun, isn't it?

Yes, you had a really good idea!

THE ROCK CONCERT
搖滾演唱會

這晚，班哲文和潘朵拉想我帶他們去聽演唱會，我本來不太想去，因為我習慣早睡早起。但為了答謝柏蒂請我看音樂劇，我決定帶大家去看Sweet Top Rock的演唱會！

1

2 Hi, Patty, it's me!

Hello, who's speaking?

Do you know that the Sweet Top Rock group are playing at the Tortiglione Theatre tonight?

3 Hi, Geronimo, it's great to hear from you!

4

6

Really? Pity I haven't got the tickets!

5

I've bought four tickets. We'll go with Benjamin and Pandora!

Yes, see you tonight!

See you there tonight at nine o'clock!

7 Thanks, Geronimo!

9

8

 14

★ 試用英語説出：「我們今晚九點見面。」

答案：*See you there tonight at nine o'clock.*

我們來到演奏廳，這時演唱會還沒開始，但台上已擺放好了各種各樣的樂器和音響器材。孩子們趁着這個機會逐一問我這些物品的英文名稱該怎麼說，你也跟着一起學習吧！

LET'S GO TO THE CINEMA!
一起去看電影！

見面聚會的機會陸續有來！這次班哲文打電話邀請潘朵拉一起去看電影！

Benjamin: Hi, Pandora, would you like to go to the cinema?

Pandora: Oh, yes, of course. To see what film?

Benjamin: An adventure film! I'll call Uncle Geronimo and Aunt Patty, too!

Pandora: Yes, let's all go to the cinema together! I'm very happy!

Benjamin: Hi, Uncle Geronimo. I've invited Pandora and Aunt Patty to the cinema. Will you come with us?

Geronimo: Ok, good idea. What time does the film start?

Benjamin: At twenty to six. Will you be there? Please, don't be late!

Geronimo: All right, see you later!

 試用英語說出以下的句子：

1. 你想去看電影嗎？

2. 哦，是的，當然了。看什麼電影呢？

答案：1. Would you like to go to the cinema? 2. Oh, yes, of course. To see what film?

 16

為了確保能買到電影票，柏蒂提前去了電影院。
幸好有她提前到，因為這次我幾乎遲到了……

Four tickets for auditorium one, please!

Here you are. It's 250 dollars all together.

看完電影後，我們一邊走出電影院，
一邊談論着剛才那套電影。

Did you like the film?
你喜歡這套電影嗎？

Pandora, do you prefer going to the cinema or to the theatre?

I prefer going to the cinema!

Did you like the film?

Yes I did, very much!

AT THE NATURAL SCIENCE MUSEUM 自然科學博物館

今天，柏蒂要帶潘朵拉去參觀自然科學博物館，那裏有一個恐龍展！於是潘朵拉打電話給班哲文邀請他一起去，當然還有我啦！

Hi, Benjamin, how are you?

Well, thanks! Aunt Patty is taking me to the Natural Science Museum.

I'm fine, and you?

Yes, of course! I'll call Uncle Geronimo, too, and we'll be right there!

We're going to see an exhibition on dinosaurs. Would you like to come, too?

It's the biggest dinosaur ever found.

How big was this dinosaur when it was alive?

Look at the drawing on that poster!

自然科學博物館裏有一家書店，裏面有很多關於恐龍的有趣圖書，其中一些圖書是由卡文娜‧淘古鼠寫的，她是這家博物館的館長，也是我的好朋友。

BOOKSHOP

magazines

books

bookshelves

poster

dinosaur

dinosaur skeleton

bookmarks

A SONG FOR YOU!

Track 2

At the Museum

At the Natural Science Museum
there is a skeleton
of a prehistoric dinosaur.
you want to know more about it
read a book!
Remember, remember
the more you read
the more you learn,
reading is wonderful
studying is wonderful!

Visiting museums is interesting
it's like plunging into the past.
If you want to know more about it
in books you'll find the answers to
your questions.
Remember, remember the more you read
the more you learn, reading is wonderful
studying is wonderful!

〈休息時間變了艱苦工作〉

在第一山上正在舉行一年一度的節日慶典：有各種各樣有趣的遊戲和美食。

班哲文：我們打算怎樣度過這一天的假期呢？

菲：緩步跑以保持身材健美，然後坐上飛機，欣賞全城風景。

謝利連摩：菲，你別生氣，不過⋯⋯

班哲文和潘朵拉：今天會舉行世界上最大的乳酪頒獎典禮。

謝利連摩：對極了！

菲：那好吧，我自己去！

謝利連摩：我要為那個傑作寫一份報告。

謝利連摩：嘩！

賴皮：這的確很美麗。看，這裏有一小片……

潘朵拉：呀……它不是一小片……

班哲文：它其實是一塊小楔子用來固定這塊乳酪的。

賴皮：呀！

謝利連摩：呀呀呀！！！

羣眾：謝—利—連—摩！謝—利—連—摩！
班哲文：叔叔，快點擺脫它！
謝利連摩：噓！向右跑？

謝利連摩：噓！噗！不，不要呀！噓！向左跑？

謝利連摩：這也不是一個好主意！我只能一直向前跑！

謝利連摩：哦，不，前面是一堵牆！現在怎麼辦？

菲：來吧，抓住它！
謝利連摩：啊？

謝利連摩：嘩！

菲：你現在安全了！
謝利連摩：沒錯，但那乳酪將被撞得粉碎！

菲：真可惜！

菲：你現在打算寫什麼？
謝利連摩：哦，那就簡單了⋯⋯

The End

謝利連摩：我會寫關於歷史上的第一場乳酪雨。

TEST 小測驗

⭐ 1. 用英語説出以下樂器或音響器材的名稱。

(a) 電結他   **(b)** 咪高峯   **(c)** 電子琴   **(d)** 低音結他

⭐ 2. 用英語説出下面的句子。

(a) 我喜歡打鼓。

I like ... ...

(b) 我比較喜歡古典音樂。

I ... ...

⭐ 3. 潘朵拉和班哲文正在通電話，用英語説出他們的對話。

喂，你是哪位？
Hello, who's ... ?

你好，潘朵拉，
是我，班哲文。
Hi, ... , ... ,
Benjamin.

你好，班哲文，你好嗎？
Hi, ... , how ... ... ?

我很好，謝謝，你呢？
I'm ... , ... , and ... ?

⭐ 4. 「很高興聽到你的聲音！」用英語該怎麼説？圈出相應的英文句子。

(a) It's nice to hear from you!

(b) See you later!

DICTIONARY 詞典

A

a long time ago　從前

adventure　冒險

amplifier　擴音器

annual　一年一度的

answers　答案

awake　清醒的

B

bass guitar　低音結他

　　（普：低音吉他）

biggest　最大的

bill　節目單

booked　預訂

bookmarks　書籤

books　書

bookshelves　書架

bookshop　書店

box office　售票處

C

cashier　收銀員

central　中間的

ceremony　典禮

cinema　電影院

classical　經典

concert　演唱會

costume　服裝

country　國家

crown　王冠

D

dancer　舞蹈員

defeated　打敗

dinosaur　恐龍

dinosaur skeleton　恐龍骨架

drums　鼓

E

easy　簡單

electric guitar　電結他
　　（普：電吉他）

enchanted　施了魔法的

exhibition　展覽

F

fairy　仙子

famous　著名的

fell asleep　睡着了

festival　節日

film　電影

first row　第一排

forest　森林

friends　朋友

G

games　遊戲

generous　大方

ghost　鬼

H

happiness　快樂

hear　聽見

history　歷史

I

imagination　幻想

invite　邀請

J

jogging　緩步跑

K

keyboards　電子琴

king　國王

kingdom　王國

L

late　遲到

lighting technician
　　燈光技術員

26

lights　燈光

M

magazines　雜誌

make-up　化妝

mask　面具

masterpiece　傑作

microphone　咪高峯
　　（普：麥克風）

miss　錯過

mixer　混音器

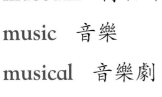

museum　博物館

music　音樂

musical　音樂劇

N

natural　自然的

O

of course　當然

P

pass　傳達

pixie　小精靈

playbill　節目單

poster　海報

prehistoric　史前的

Q

queen　王后

questions　問題

R

relatives　親戚

report　報告

returned　回到

rock　搖滾樂

S

safe　安全

scene　布景

school play　學校話劇

science　科學

script　劇本

seats　座位

set　布景

singing　唱歌

sound technician

　音響技術員

spell　咒語

spirit of the forest　森林精靈

spotlights　射燈

start　開始

wise　聰明

witch　女巫

worry　擔心

T

telephone　電話

thanks　多謝

theatre　劇院

tickets　票

together　一起

W

wedge　楔子

28

看在一千塊莫澤雷勒乳酪的份上，你學得開心嗎？很開心，對不對？好極了！跟你一起跳舞唱歌我也很開心！我等着你下次繼續跟班哲文和潘朵拉一起玩一起學英語呀。現在要說再見了，當然是用英語說啦！

GERONIMO'S ISLAND
老鼠島地圖

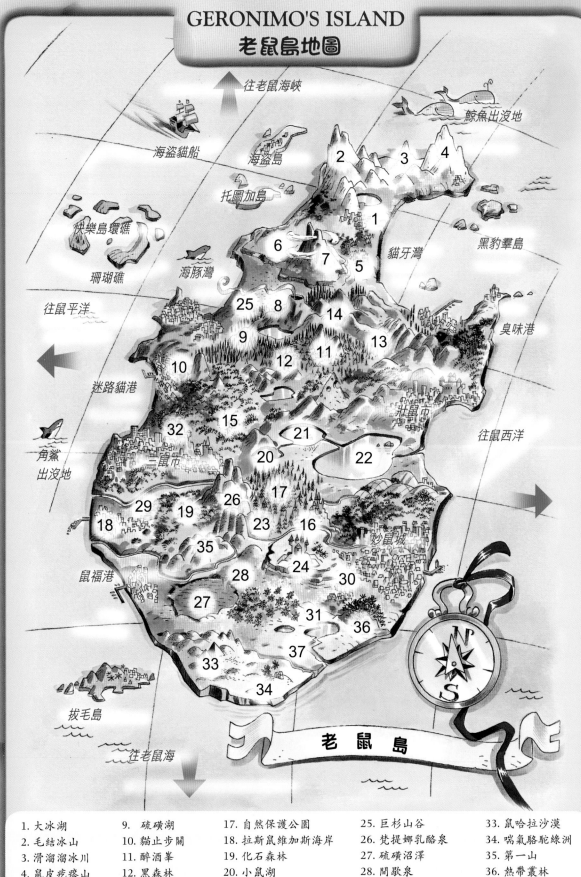

往老鼠海峽

鯨魚出沒地

海盜貓船

海盜島

托圖加島

黑豹羣島

快樂島環礁

珊瑚礁

海豚灣

貓牙灣

臭味港

往鼠平洋

迷路貓港

往鼠西洋

角鯊
出沒地

壯鼠市

三鼠市

妙鼠城

鼠福港

拔毛島

往老鼠海

老 鼠 島

1. 大冰湖	9. 硫磺湖	17. 自然保護公園	25. 巨杉山谷	33. 鼠哈拉沙漠
2. 毛結冰山	10. 貓止步關	18. 拉斯鼠維加斯海岸	26. 梵提娜乳酪泉	34. 喘氣駱駝綠洲
3. 滑溜溜冰川	11. 醉酒峯	19. 化石森林	27. 硫磺沼澤	35. 第一山
4. 鼠皮疙瘩山	12. 黑森林	20. 小鼠湖	28. 間歇泉	36. 熱帶叢林
5. 鼠基斯坦	13. 吸血鬼谷	21. 中鼠湖	29. 田鼠谷	37. 蚊子谷
6. 鼠坦尼亞	14. 發冷山	22. 大鼠湖	30. 瘋鼠谷	
7. 吸血鬼山	15. 黑影關	23. 諾比奧拉乳酪峯	31. 蚊子沼澤	
8. 鐵板鼠火山	16. 客嗇鼠城堡	24. 肯尼貓城堡	32. 史卓奇諾乳酪城堡	

Geronimo Stilton

EXERCISE BOOK

練習冊

想知道自己對 FREE TIME 掌握了多少，
趕快打開後面的練習完成它吧！

ENGLISH!

21 **FREE TIME** 課餘時間

THE TELEPHONE IS RINGING
電話響了

⭐ 柏蒂打電話給謝利連摩邀請他一起去看學校話劇。從下面選出正確的答案填在橫線上，完成他們的對話。

> of course   relatives   school play   Invite
> this afternoon   Pass the word round

1. Are you coming to see Benjamin and

   Pandora's _____ ?

2. Yes, _____ !

3. _____ ,

   Geronimo! _____

   friends and _____ .

4. Ok, Patty! See you _____

   _____ !

THE SCHOOL PLAY
學校話劇

⭐ 學校話劇開演了，根據每個小朋友的造型，猜猜他們正在扮演什麼角色，從下面選出正確的詞彙填在圖畫旁的橫線上。

dancer	king	witch
queen	fairy	pixie

THE ENCHANTED FOREST

1.  _____

2.  _____

3.  _____

4.  _____

5.  _____

6.  _____

WHOSE IS THIS?
這是誰的？

⭐ 根據下面的圖畫，他們在說什麼？選出適當的句子，把代表答案的英文字母填在句框裏。

A. It's mine.　　　　B. Whose hat is this?
C. They are mine.　　D. This crown is mine!
E. Whose are these leaves?

THE MUSICAL 音樂劇

⭐ 謝利連摩、柏蒂、班哲文和潘朵拉一起去看音樂劇。根據圖畫，從下面選出正確的詞彙填在橫線上，完成他們的對話。

they　　seats　　tickets　　idea　　Fun　　row

1. Good evening, I booked four _____ over the phone!

2. Yes, here _____ are!

3. What number are our _____ ?

4. They are in the first _____ , central seats, 13, 14, 15 and 16!

5. _____ , isn't it?

6. Yes, you had a really good _____ !

4

THE ROCK CONCERT
搖滾演唱會

⭐ 你認識下面這些樂器和音響器材的英文名稱嗎？從下面選出正確的詞彙填在圖畫旁的橫線上。

acoustic guitar	microphone	mixer
bass guitar	keyboards	drums
electric guitar	lights	

1.  _____

2.  _____

3.  _____

4. _____

5. _____

6. _____

7.  _____

8.  _____

LET'S GO TO THE CINEMA!
一起去看電影！

⭐ 1. 柏蒂到電影院去買票。根據圖畫，從下面選出正確的詞彙填在填線上。

(a) _____ (b) _____ (c) _____

playbill

auditorium

cashier

⭐ 2. 謝利連摩、柏蒂和孩子們正在談論他們剛才看過的電影。從下面選出正確的詞彙填在橫線上，完成他們的對話。

| theatre | film | prefer | much |

(a) Did you like the _____ ?

(b) Yes I did, very _____ !

(c) Pandora, do you prefer going to the cinema or to the _____ ?

(d) I _____ going to the cinema!

AT THE NATURAL SCIENCE MUSEUM 自然科學博物館

⭐ 卡文娜・淘古鼠正在向謝利連摩和潘朵拉介紹關於恐龍的展覽。從下面選出正確的詞彙填在橫線上，完成句子。

poster	alive	drawing
found	big	dinosaur

1. It's the biggest _____ ever _____ .

2. How _____ was this dinosaur when it was _____ ?

3. Look at the _____ on that _____ !

ANSWERS 答案

TEST 小測驗

1. (a) electric guitar   (b) microphone   (c) keyboards   (d) bass guitar

2. (a) I like <u>playing the drums</u>.   (b) I <u>prefer classical music</u>.

3. Pan: Hello, who's <u>speaking</u>?

   Ben: Hi, <u>Pandora</u>, <u>it's me</u>, Benjamin.

   Pan: Hi, <u>Benjamin</u>, how <u>are you</u>?

   Ben: I'm <u>fine</u>, <u>thanks</u>, and <u>you</u>?

4. It's nice to hear from you!

EXERCISE BOOK 練習冊

P.1

1. school play   2. of course   3. Pass the word round, Invite, relatives   4. this afternoon

P.2

1. king   2. queen   3. fairy   4. witch   5. pixie   6. dancer

P.3

1. B   2. A   3. E   4. C   5. D

P.4

1. tickets   2. they   3. seats   4. row   5. Fun   6. idea

P.5

1. electric guitar   2. bass guitar   3. drums   4. microphone   5. mixer   6. lights

7. acoustic guitar   8. keyboards

P.6

1. (a) auditorium   (b) playbill   (c) cashier

2. (a) film   (b) much   (c) theatre   (d) prefer

P.7

1. dinosaur, found   2. big, alive   3. drawing, poster